# Hello Mum

Bernardine Evaristo's four novels are: *Blonde Roots*, *Soul Tourists*, *The Emperor's Babe* and *Lara*. She lives in London and received an MBE for Services to Literature in 2009. Visit her website at *www.bevaristo.net* or her blog at *www.bevaristo. wordpress.com*.

# Hello Mum

Bernardine Evaristo

PENGUIN BOOKS

PENGUIN BOOKS

Published by the Penguin Group
Penguin Books Ltd, 80 Strand, London WC2R ORL, England
Penguin Group (USA) Inc., 375 Hudson Street, New York, New York 10014, USA
Penguin Group (Canada), 90 Eglinton Avenue East, Suite 700, Toronto, Ontario, Canada M4P 2Y3
(a division of Pearson Penguin Canada Inc.)
Penguin Ireland, 25 St Stephen's Green, Dublin 2, Ireland
(a division of Penguin Books Ltd)
Penguin Group (Australia), 250 Camberwell Road, Camberwell, Victoria 3124, Australia
(a division of Pearson Australia Group Pty Ltd)
Penguin Books India Pvt Ltd, 11 Community Centre, Panchsheel Park, New Delhi – 110 017, India
Penguin Group (NZ), 67 Apollo Drive, Rosedale, North Shore 0632, New Zealand
(a division of Pearson New Zealand Ltd)
Penguin Books (South Africa) (Pty) Ltd, 24 Sturdee Avenue, Rosebank,
Johannesburg 2196, South Africa

Penguin Books Ltd, Registered Offices: 80 Strand, London WC2R ORL, England

www.penguin.com

First published 2010
1

Set in Stone Serif 12/16 pt
Typeset by Palimpsest Book Production Limited, Grangemouth, Stirlingshire
Printed in England by Clays Ltd, St Ives plc

ISBN: 978–0–141–04438–5

www.greenpenguin.co.uk

Mixed Sources
Product group from well-managed
forests and other controlled sources
www.fsc.org  Cert no. SA-COC-1592
© 1996 Forest Stewardship Council
FSC

Penguin Books is committed to a sustainable future
for our business, our readers and our planet.
The book in your hands is made from paper
certified by the Forest Stewardship Council.

For the children . . .

# Contents

# Chapter One

# The Estate

Hello Mum,

I knew some madness was gonna kick off that day. As I walked through the estate it was so hot I thought the tarmac would melt and my feet sink into the road. Serious! I thought the air would burst into flames and the parked cars explode like bombs.

Within minutes my jeans, T-shirt and socks stuck to me like that disgusting hair grease you use and all I wanted was to wrap my hands around a nice, cold can of Coke from the shops.

When I complained about the heat that morning you said you was gonna buy me shorts and sandals from Primark, which made me crack up. Mum, shorts and sandals? What planet are you on? Yeah, if I was like, five, yeah? I'd get beaten up before I even reached the high street. By my own boys too, for bringing shame on them.

Everyone was escaping their boiling hot flats

that afternoon and everyone looked up when a police helicopter began to circle noisily in the sky. It was like a mosquito you wanted to squash but couldn't reach. At night their red beams swooped down like they was hunting animals when all I was doing was just standing around chatting nonsense with my boys. It was pure pressure, ya get me?

I looked up at the top-floor balconies and wondered when the next person would chuck themselves off. Thump! The postman found the last one. I made up lyrics about it: *Another man down/ Blood on the ground/ Lost then found/ Get used to the sound. /Another man down/ Don't stick around/ You can't take flight/ Suicide Heights.*

I used to lie in my room at night expecting to see dead bodies falling outside my window like in films.

Nice place I had to live in. Thanks.

Geriatrics were shading themselves on the lower balconies underneath lines of washing. You used to say, 'Old people are vulnerable, be kind to them.' No way! I tell you, they hated teenagers. Given half the chance, they'd burn us all in gas ovens like Hitler. No doubt!

One time I was standing by the bins with my boys when that old man from No. 32 came up to dump his black rubbish bag. He wore a dirty old man's coat even though it was summer. He was stooped and short so all you could see was his bald head with brown spots on it like tea stains. Then, when he turned to leave, he whacked my legs with his walking stick. Can you believe it? I hadn't done nothing, yeah? It hurt too. I should've whacked him back. Delmar spat at him and I shouted out I'd tell the police he tried to touch me up. Plenty witnesses, man! Plenty witnesses! We all jeered *'Paedo!'* as he hobbled off.

Girls in short skirts with legs like burnt sausages were dancing outside one of the ground-floor flats. Rihanna's 'Disturbia' was blasting out from a sound system. Like they were in a hip hop video or something. *Not!* It disturbia'd me, I tell you. Bunch of wannabes. They was covered in that face crap girls wear to hide the fact that they're dogs. The dance was called the Migraine Skank. You put your hands over your ears as if you've got a headache, then shake your head from side to side while bending over. I got a headache just looking at them. Pure stupidness!

I hoped Shontelle wouldn't turn out like them. I think Shontelle was the best thing in my life. I know it sounds sissy but I loved it when she fell asleep on my lap and I had to carry her to bed without waking her. You love her too, Mum. More than me 'cos she was no trouble. Don't lie!

Youngers were kicking a football about like they was in the World Cup final. Brazil versus Italy. A car window was just waiting to be smashed in. You'd blame them, go on about kids being vandals these days, but not me. Where else was they gonna play? Every little kid had been warned that the park next door was full of perverts and child murderers. So they weren't allowed inside. A big park and it was empty. Nice one.

'Awright, JJ?' a couple of them called out. Micky and Derrick. About eight years old, I reckon. I nodded back, hands in pockets. I was starting to get their respect. It felt good.

You used to talk about the good old days in the 1980s when you'd spend the whole summer playing in the park pretending it was the countryside. The good old days before the youth club was shut down and they organized things for you and your mates to do.

The good old days when the estate was new and before the riots happened that you said ruined everything.

The good old days when you had no son called Jerome to make your life a misery.

So if the 1980s was the good old days, that meant I lived in the bad new days, right?

Mum, this is what my life was like, and for once, you can't answer back.

# Chapter Two

# Home

My room wasn't a room, it was a cupboard. If I stood in the middle of it and stretched my arms out I could touch both walls. As I got taller, the room got smaller.

There wasn't even space for drawers or a wardrobe, and I was so fed up having to stuff my clothes and old teddies on them wonky shelves you put up on the walls. (Yeah, yeah, in a heap, whatever.)

'Tidy your room, Jerome,' you'd moan, as if *you* lived in it and not *me*. Like, what's the point making my bed in the morning when it's gonna get messed up again at night? Pure madness!

When Delmar came round I had to hide the teddies in that baggy woollen jumper you bought for me last birthday. Mum, no one wears *jumpers*.

Oh and before I forget, say hello to Barnaby the One-Eyed Bandit for me! You'll find him in the jumper. LOL! That means laugh out loud. LMAO means laughing my arse off. You know what? We lived in the same flat but we didn't even speak the same language. You was always going on at me, 'Why don't you speak properly any more, Jerome?'

Mum, you had no idea what my life was like. No way could I speak all la-di-dah like Harry Potter and survive in this hood. Every time I opened my mouth I'd get beaten up.

My bedroom's still the same, isn't it? My things are still there, aren't they? You haven't thrown them away? That's like throwing me away.

I bet you have. You have, haven't you? I bet you've given my room to Shontelle and taken down my *Scarface* poster. The wickedest film ever made, man. Al Pacino playing the great gangsta Tony Montana. He was my hero and everyone else's too. Why? Obvious! He was a nobody who became a somebody. He did what he had to do and by the way, you're the *only* person in the world who hated that film. I swear!

Remember how I liked to watch *MTV Cribs* on the telly? All those rappers' Hollywood-style homes with big white walls and massive posters of *Scarface*, yeah? They'd have fridges the size of our kitchen and bathrooms bigger than our sitting room. Chill-out room, games room, recording studio, study – with no books in it (ya get me?). Gardens the size of a football pitch. Garages with enough cars lined up outside. BMW, Mercedes, Rolls-Royce Phantom, Lamborghini Roadster. Hummer H2, Mercedes-Benz SLR McLaren, Porsche GT3, Aston Martin DB9, Ferrari 360.

I wanted it all. 'Course I did. Everyone does. That's a fact. Get rich or die trying, as my man 50 Cent said. Big house, plenty dollar, expensive cars. *That's* what I'm talking about!

We didn't even have a flat-screen telly, which was embarrassing when Delmar came round.

And another thing, Mum, you was always going on at me to work harder at school but you hated my lyrics. Like, if I'd have called it poetry you'd have told the whole world. Put on that posh voice you used at Parents' Evening at school.

'Jerome writes poetry. Isn't my boy clever?'

You was well proud of me when I came top of the class my last year at primary school. I think that was the last time I did anything you liked. I didn't mind you putting the trophy over the fireplace then, but it was embarrassing when I got older. Not cool, Mum. Not cool. By the end of my first year at secondary school I stopped being the class creep and dropped down to No. 17 out of twenty-nine pupils. You went ballistic.

Typical school report: 'Jerome can do well when he puts his mind to it, but he's easily distracted.'

Check this, Mumsy. You can't be a nerd at secondary school and be liked by the people who count. You can't waste your time reading books when you're a teenager, either. That's for when I'm old, like you. Oh, I forgot, happy birthday for last Sunday. You might be thirty-four but you don't look a day over forty. Jokes, man. Jokes! I did make you laugh, though. Mos def (most definitely). Don't lie. I did.

Anyway, you can talk. If you hadn't left university 'cos you was pregnant with me, you could've become a schoolteacher like you wanted. Then we'd live in a proper house with a garden and everything.

If I had to write a school report for you it would go like this: 'Kimisi Cole-Wallace could have done well, but she was easily distracted.' LMAO!

Listen, I had to escape our dump that afternoon. Shontelle was watching cartoons in the sitting room. Sometimes I joined her just 'cos she made me laugh when she got so excited at all the silliness on the telly, but I wasn't in the mood that day. And you was in the kitchen frying onions and garlic so the whole flat stank. You knew I hated the smell of garlic so why didn't you close the kitchen door? I was suffocating to death in my cupboard what with the heat.

And you know that window only opened out a crack in case I fell out when I was a kid. Except I wasn't a kid no more, right? So why didn't you get the council to fix it?

And another thing, how did you expect me to stay in that roasting prison cell all the time? I could only walk fourteen steps in the whole flat?

Then, when I told you I was going out, you started giving me a hard time as usual. One minute you was saying I was the man of the house, the next you wanted me on curfew.

'I'm off, Mum. See you later.'

'You think so? That depends on whether I bolt the door or not, doesn't it?'

'Oh c'mon, don't start. I'll be back soon.'

'Soon never comes soon enough, with *you*.'

'What time you want me back, then?'

'Nine o'clock. If you're a minute late you can sleep in the hallway outside. Why? Because I for one will not be moving *my* butt from *my* sofa in the middle of *my* film to unbolt *my* door to *my* tearaway son.'

'Well, seeing as I'm giving you so much grief I might as well leave home, yeah?'

'Is that a big fourteen-year-old man talking? Can't even grow a beard yet. Can't vote, can't leave school, can't drive a car, can't drink, can't smoke, can't rent a flat, can't open a bank account without my permission. Can't leave the country without my permission, can't do anything, in fact, without my permission. So where are you going to go, exactly? Sleep rough on the streets with those dirty, drunk, druggy homeless people out there? You go on and have a nice life, dear.'

'Plenty places actually! Delmar will sort me out.'

'What? That boy is close friends with the devil. You be back by nine or I'll ground you for two weeks! It's time you began to listen to your mother and stop your *damn* rudeness!'

'Yeah, yeah, whatever!'

Bam! I slammed the front door and leapt down the stairs three at a time with some new lyrics forming in my head. *Reality must be found/ Don't get pushed around/ Stand up for your rights/ Fight, fight wiv all your might.*

I'm surprised that door didn't break the number of times I slammed it. You was always stressing me out. You could make me angrier than anyone else in the world. You was ruining my life with all your moaning. I couldn't wait to be older and do things *my* way.

# Chapter Three

## Area Codes

Once I'd reached the edge of our estate I wasn't so angry. I was just relieved to be outside and away from the flat that you wanted to make my prison.

I turned the corner of Mandela House and was stepping out on to the pavement. The B-Block Boys was larking about outside Brampton Estate opposite. Cutting through their end was the quickest way to the shops. Big problem, though. It's in a different area code so I couldn't even cross to their side of the road or they'd rush me (beat me up).

I watched them out of the corner of my eye. I counted nine of them about my age and a bit older. Tyrone was there too. He was seventeen, always wore black and was built like an army tank. If you saw him on the street you moved out of his way or he'd just roll over you. Tyrone had this killer bang: knock you out in one punch.

Ba dum! He'd tried it on this sixth-former called Patrice at school who was giving him looks in the playground. Mum, Patrice was eighteen and not small either. He was laid flat out on the ground. I was there. I saw it with my own two eyes. After that, everyone kept well clear of Tyrone except his crew.

If they saw me looking they might ask me what I was looking at and then I'd be for it. Especially if they was looking for a buzz. No back-up, neither. I never relaxed. Never. Look sharp, Jerome, I always told myself. Be on guard at all times. Keep your mouth shut and your eyes wide open. You never know who's gonna jump you.

There wasn't even any beef between my crew and the B-Block Boys. It's just how it was. They had their ends to represent and we had ours. Representing or 'repping your ends', that's what we did. Your 'ends' was your area code. You know, what you old-fashioned people call a postcode.

I know you didn't know about area codes. I wasn't gonna tell you, either, or you'd whinge even more about me going out.

Look Mum, *you* might have called the road in between the two estates Redcross Street but we called it the Front Line. *You* might have been able to cut through Brampton Estate to the shops, but I couldn't. *You* might have thought they were just a group of kids wasting time when they should be studying. To me they was the B-Block Boys.

This is how it played out.

We lived in NW14 and over the road was NW15, which made it out of bounds. Same all over London. If you live in SW9, don't go minding your business in E5 because they'll make *your* business *their* business. If you live in W12, stay away from W11 unless you want to get mashed up. Girls too. Delmar's sister Delice got rushed by a gang of girls 'cos she slipped into their ends at Stamford Hill, even though she was with a friend who lived there. Hospital for three weeks and had her jaw wired up, didn't she? When she was better, her mum shipped her off to live with her granny in Barbados.

To be honest, it was safer to leave London than move across it.

You asked me why I stopped going to visit Auntie Olivette in Camberwell unless you dragged me there. You wanna hear the truth? Okay.

The last time I went to see her I went into McDonald's on my way home. I was in the queue minding my own business looking forward to a quarterpounder with fries, strawberry milkshake and apple pie for afters. You know Auntie Olivette with her brown rice and pumpkin seeds vomit-food. I was starving 'cos I'd told her I'd already eaten. I was gonna blow all my week's pocket money on some proper food. Couldn't wait.

Suddenly a voice behind me said, 'Yo, blud. What ends you from?' I turned around and three Olders aged about twenty stood right behind me. They had mean looks that told me they'd slash my face to ribbons with a knife if I so much as blinked the wrong way. Afterwards, they'd calmly eat a cheeseburger as if nothing had happened. They was wearing yellow bandannas underneath their grey baseball caps, a sign they were members of the Camberwell Campaign, one of the most famous gangs in London. Half their boys were inside for stabbing up some boys. I tell you, I felt so much shivers, Mum.

It was when I was twelve, Mum, but you know I looked older 'cos I was so tall. They probably thought I was some sixteen-year-old gangsta or something. That's why bus drivers made me hand over my bus pass to check it wasn't fake. That's what they made out, anyway. Why is it that everywhere I went people treated me like a criminal? Bus drivers hated me. The Fedz hated me. The men in the corner shop hated me – even when I went in alone, one of them followed me around. They always checked my notes, too. Making a big show of it, holding it up to the light.

You told me they followed you around as well, and you're a grown-up. I would never steal, Mum. You taught me not to. See, I did listen to you sometimes, when you made sense. I didn't want to end up in one of them youth offending places.

When I walked on the street, girls and women crossed the road too, as if I was going to snatch their bags or stab them. That started from when I was about eleven. Every time a police car passed, it slowed down and the Fedz eyeballed me, even in daylight when I was alone. I'd been stop-and-searched four times too. The newspapers hated me. The television news hated me. Everyone hated me, except my family and my crew. You know what? All I ever got was total disrespect. Sometimes I thought, if everyone thinks I'm a scumbag criminal, I'll be a scumbag criminal, innit?

Back in McDonald's I gave the gangstas Auntie Olivette's street as my address. It was the only road I knew in Camberwell. I told them I'd just moved into the area 'cos my mum had died of cancer and my dad was banged up for murder in the slammer. I hoped that would get me both sympathy and respect. It was a stupid lie and I was sure they'd just laugh at it. Especially as my voice was trembling as if someone had turned me upside down and was shaking me by my legs.

Shame, shame and more shame. They didn't look sorry or scared, though, but just pushed up in my face and stared at me really hard until my eyes started to water. Oh, more shame.

'Yeah, well, watch yourself,' the middle one said. Then they turned and did that limp-shuffle out the door, bumping people with their shoulders. It did look stupid, I admit. Remember when I started walking like that you said to me, 'Jerome, you do not have one leg shorter than the other, so why don't you walk like a normal person?' I listened to you. See, good boy really, Mumsy-Wumsy.

I stayed in McDonald's three hours in case they were waiting outside to rush me. Then I ran all the way to the Oval to get the tube. I thought my legs would collapse, not from running but from fear. By the time I got to the station my clothes was soaked.

All the way home I kept looking at the tube door in case they jumped in.

It was a warning but I wasn't listening.

# Chapter Four

# The Deptford Warriors

I never told you about the time I went to a party down South London. It was about a year after my McDonald's warning. You thought me and Adrian was downstairs on the estate all night chatting nonsense as usual. Time to fess up. I wasn't.

We went to his cousin Michael's party in Deptford. His parents had gone to an emergency funeral in Ghana and left Michael alone in the house. What else was a nineteen-year-old student gonna do but have a party? We took a bus to Tottenham Court Road, then a tube to London Bridge and then a train to Deptford. We were so excited, like little kids on an adventure. We were mucking about on the tube hanging from the rails and doing fly kicks as high as we could go. I won 'cos Adrian's legs was too short. No one told us off or nothing. They probably thought we was hoodies and were scared we'd mug them and stuff.

The party was in a house with a garden full of trees and bushes and everything. I know what you're thinking. Did they have a plasma telly, Jerome? Yep, they did.

The house was full of Michael's mates and their girls all catching joke and skanking to Snoop Dog, Jay-Z, Busta Rhymes and some African rap that wasn't as bad as you'd think.

I didn't touch any drink, though, Mum. They had a fridge full of beers and bottles and rum and whisky on the sideboard. Well, seeing as I'm fessing up, I did try some whisky but I knocked it back like it was water. Big mistake! My mouth felt like I'd eaten one of those small red chillies raw. I hopped about on one leg like a madman and Adrian cracked up. How can anyone like that stuff?

Me and Adrian felt like grown-ups for the first time. Hanging with the Olders. We were the youngest there and stuffing ourselves with some well-nice Ghana food Michael's girl Ama had cooked. Peanut and chicken stew and something called foo-foo that looked a bit like that disgusting porridge you're always trying to get me to eat, but tasted way better. *Not* difficult.

So check this now, me and Adrian was in the kitchen alone. It faced the street. We was stuffing ourselves, like I said. Suddenly this person showed at the window in a black hoodie with a black scarf around his face. All you could see were his eyes. Mum, I nearly screamed like a girl in those old horror films you like to watch. We raced out and told Michael and by the time he and his mates ran in, there was a gang out there. They was all blacked-out from top to toe which meant they were gonna cause some damage. They was banging on the front door and kitchen window and waving knives. It was like being in Iraq or somewhere. I almost threw up my food, honestly.

Michael told everyone they were the Deptford Warriors. They was annoyed 'cos they'd not been invited to his party even though it was private. I know you don't like swearing but I just thought, WTF! (What The F*ck!) Michael wasn't in no gang. He had no beef with that gang. He was just having his mates round. Michael wasn't a rough-neck type. He was like Adrian, a bit soft, and he spoke posh too.

He called the Fedz but said they wouldn't even bother to come. But they did, like five minutes later, tops, and their sirens was blaring. The gang ran off.

So now what? Me and Adrian had to get home, innit? Everyone else wanted to leave too so we left as a big group but soon split off to get buses and trains. We walked to the train station with about ten others from the party. Adrian and I made sure we was in the middle.

Then the madness kicked off. The Deptford Warriors had been waiting and as we was walking down Deptford High Street, they came towards us with knives and baseball bats. About fifteen of them. Black hoods up, faces covered. Before I knew it I felt a baseball bat smack down on my head. I was so shocked and dazed but it didn't knock me out. I don't know how we got out of that scrum but me and Adrian just turned and ran as if we were competing in the school sprint race. At least I did, Adrian was dragging behind me so I had to slow down. (Too much fish and chips, Ade!)

At the top of the high street we turned left and ran up a hill for ages, cars shooting past us, until we came to a massive open park with massive white houses all around it. We opened the gate of one of them big houses. It had massive white columns by the front door like in ancient Greece from 500 years ago. (History, Year 5!) The windows didn't have no curtains and I could see a room with big white walls and high ceilings like in the museums the school forced us to visit. On one wall was a massive painting of red and black splotches that was totally ugly. On the other was bookshelves stuffed with books. I bet they were teachers. And very old. No doubt!

We crept into the front garden and crouched behind some prickly rose bushes.

It was then that I really felt the bump on my head. It hurt like no one's business. No blood, though, thank God. I did too. Thank God, that is, you'll be pleased to hear. Maybe he saved my life? The next day I had a headache and half a tennis ball on top of my head but my hair covered it. Just as well I was growing an Afro. (Yeah, you complained about that too!) Check this now, though, I couldn't believe it when Adrian started crying. Not little tears but big sobs like a baby, a cry-baby. I told him to shut up or the people in the house would hear him. So he put his fist in his mouth but still went on crying like he couldn't stop. He shoulda been a man like me. I thought, if I was jumped by someone, Adrian would run away and save himself. I'd have no protection. My boy was a wimp.

He wanted to stay there all night, but I looked over the wall and realized we was all right in that spot. The lights in the house was on but unless they had dogs we were well hidden. We'd left the Deptford Warriors' end and was in some place where rich people lived. I'd never seen so much rich houses in my life. Massive plasma tellys in every one of them. I would have bet £10 on it. Swear down!

We walked across the park and it was like being in the countryside of your good old days. Not that I've ever been to the countryside properly. I remember we saw it from the train when you took me to Brighton for the day when I was a kid.

We came to a bus stop and I saw we was somewhere called Blackheath Common. We got the first bus out of there and asked the bus driver how to get to London Bridge.

It was dark but still only, like, ten o'clock. Every time Adrian tried to talk to me on the way home I just ignored him. My boy was always a motor-mouth. Now he was really jarring me like a childish younger brother.

The next day he found out that some of Michael's mates got stabbed up. They did some damage too. The police arrived quickly and no one died. That's why the Deptford Warriors didn't chase us. The Olders fought back.

Now you know. I was where I shouldn't have been. My second lucky escape. I learnt my lesson that night.

Stay where it's safe, blud.

# Chapter Five

# The Wall

Adrian's dad found out he was at Michael's house somehow and he grounded him for one month, then put him under curfew. Home by 6.30 every night. No kidding! His dad said if his grades didn't get better he was gonna send Adrian home to Ghana to live with his Uncle Kojo. Adrian said over there you couldn't backchat your teachers or elders and if you did they beat you so bad you never did it again. They used canes and everything. Adrian said the kids over there was obedient 'cos they had no choice. Sounded like hell to me.

His flat was even smaller than ours and he shared a tiny bedroom with bunk beds with his brother Mark! He went crazy staying at home all the time, but he was a goody two-shoes and let his dad boss him about. I felt sorry for him.

I, me, Jerome Cole-Wallace, would never let no one boss me around, ya get me? I didn't want to be no pussy-boy like him.

23

You know how me and Adrian had been tight since primary school? Always just the two of us. Bezzie mates and all that. Everyone on our estate left us alone 'cos they thought we were just stupid geeks and didn't count. 'Cos Adrian was short and pudgy and I was tall and thin, people thought we looked funny together. You used to laugh at us too. Those two big dimples on his cheeks let him down the worst, though. (No, Mum, *not* cute!) I told him to have plastic surgery to get rid of them when he was older. No way would I be seen with dimples. *Believe!*

Remember how the summer we left primary school me and Ade sat on the wall at the bottom of our flats and pretended we was private detectives? Sometimes we was out there till 10 p.m. if it was still light. When you passed us you rolled your eyes and shook your head like we was well stupid.

We bought those plastic sunglasses from the £1 shop that looked like the glasses Horatio Caine wears in *CSI Miami*. Fake moustaches from the party shop on the high street. Old men's hats and macs from the second-hand shop. We sat there with our notebooks watching the comings and goings around us. Anything suspicious, we wrote down.

Everyone laughed at us like we was aliens from

another planet but nobody really bothered us 'cos we was too young. We couldn't do that when we went to William Holland Secondary, though. You had to grow up and act like a man.

Honestly Mum, we should have worked for the police or social services or something. When I think about it now, we did notice a lot of stuff going on that was wrong.

Like, how the woman in No. 21 left her two little kids alone inside the flat while she went to the pub. Then about two hours later she'd come home drunk with these different men. The manky kind with beer guts and greasy hair and no teeth.

Or we'd count the number of crack-heads going in and out of No. 15. Sometimes there'd be, like twenty people in one hour. Some of them looked quite ordinary, clean and everything. Others of them looked like they'd been dipped in old chip-pan fat.

One time we saw a bloke run out of No. 18 and into No. 19. About five minutes later the police arrived with two monkey vans and four cars. They jumped out and ran up the stairs to No. 18. When no one answered the door they knocked it down with that big black stick they use. Of course, he wasn't there. We noticed an unmarked police car pull up afterwards. Every two hours it drove off and another one replaced it. When we came down the next morning No. 18 was boarded up and the unmarked car was gone.

Then there was Yvonne, who was in our class but taller than the other girls and with baby boobies that we all teased her about. Me and Adrian always wrote down that her mum left the flat at 9 p.m. to go to work. She was a cleaner for London Underground. One time, soon as her mum left, Yvonne came out too, looking a bit nervous. She was wearing grown-up clothes, like a short skirt and T-shirt with a low front. She ran off out of the estate. The next morning we was on the wall at 8 a.m. and a BMW with a man inside dropped her off and she ran up to the flat just before her mum got back. She was our age, eleven. Even I knew that wasn't right.

Then there was the six wimpy art students who moved into No. 2. They used to carry those big black portfolio cases and look nervous when they walked around. I used to hear them talking in posh voices about going to exhibitions. Me and Adrian thought we'd charge them weekly 'protection money' not to burgle their flat.

Come to think of it, our heads wasn't screwed on right. We should have blackmailed half the estate. Plenty dollar!

But after that night in Deptford everything

changed. Every time I saw Adrian I just wanted to punch out his lights. I never did. I never did hit anyone. Can you believe it? Maybe in primary school, kidding around, but not when I was older. I was like that Martin Luther King from the olden days you was always going on about. Non-violent.

Adrian kept waiting for me after school to walk home together. But I saw him for what he was. A wimp and I didn't have room for no wimp in my life.

I realized my life was screwed. I had to get hard or I would be a target.

Another thing that changed was that I couldn't think clearly any more. My mind was foggy and I felt angry all the time. I punched a hole in my bedroom wall one day when you were at work, the bit where it was damp and soft. You never noticed 'cos I covered it up with a poster of 50 Cent.

Like, don't nobody mess with the JJ, yeah!

Remember you kept asking me what was wrong?

One evening when I hadn't spoken a word since I woke up and it was night-time, you went on, 'I've had it up to here with your bad moods, Jerome. You used to have them sometimes, now you have them all the damn time. What the flipping heck can be so bad? Huh? You're alive, you're well fed, you have two arms and legs and at least half a brain. Maybe I should arrange some of those anger management sessions for you. I'm sure half your school attends them anyway.'

What kind of snide comment was that? It wasn't my fault, it was yours. Like I had a choice about what school to go to anyway? I tell you, I felt like I wanted to hit you for that. Yeah, hit you. I can't believe I felt like that but I did. I went into my bedroom and slammed the door and beat up my bed instead.

What did you expect me to say? Anyway, I couldn't tell you nothing because you couldn't do nothing about it.

# Chapter Six

# The Kamikaze Kru

The weekend after Deptford I went to find Delmar and his Kamikaze Kru at their spot behind Cherry Blossom House. The Kamikaze Kru repped our end.

I heard their laughter before I turned the corner. There was about ten of them, all with bikes. Two of them doing back-wheel spins. The rest was sitting on a wall. Delmar was sitting on a broken chair someone had dumped there. His feet was on the seat and his bum on the backrest. They all went silent when I showed. Not in a bad way. They didn't give me filthy looks or nothing. More in a – what are *you* doing here – way. Every kid on the estate knew this was their hangout. Out of bounds.

I just stood there feeling stupid until Delmar finally said, 'You looking for someone or what?'

Delmar was two years above me at school but he always nodded when he saw me in the corridors. We were from the same ends, right? Everyone knew him. At fifteen he looked more like nineteen. He was a cool guy. A money-maker. He pumped up at the gym and I swear his arms were thicker than my thighs. His dad, Delroy, got life for murder when Delmar was still a baby. Everyone knew about Delroy, though word was that he was framed.

Delmar wouldn't be seen dead in anything from Primark. Labels all the way, ya get me? I always checked out what he wore. Everyone did. That day he had on a black T-shirt with 'WU TANG' written across it in big white letters. A pair of True Religion jeans with a real Gucci belt. On his feet? Brand-new, black Prada sneakers so shiny it was like they'd been dipped in glue. Those shoes made me giddy just looking at them. His diamond and gold stud earrings were real too. I'd seen them in thugfashion.com when I was cruising the net. What you'd call window-shopping, Mum. No way would they be fake, like most kids round here. The real thing. No doubt!

If I wore any of that gear I'd be mugged every day. But Delmar had built a reputation 'cos he had soldier skills. He was stuck up in his game. He had respect.

He was lucky too 'cos his older brother Dexter was legend.

Dexter! *The* Dexter!

No one messes with a bruv who wears a platinum chain so thick and heavy it needs a crane just to put it round his neck in the morning. No one messes with a bruv who drives a blacked-out BMW, ya get me? What's more, everyone knew Dexter had a 40-calibre, gold-plated pistol with silver-plated bullets he wasn't afraid to use. Don't mess with The Dexter!

I saw him sometimes when he came to visit Delmar and his mum.

Dexter was nineteen and everything he wore was black except for his bright red Kanye West LV Don trainers! Rah! Those twin babies cost about £700 a pair, if you could get them. I heard some was going for nearly £1,000. Those babies was so bright I bet they glowed in the dark like those glow-bracelets I bought for Shontelle. If you touched them your hands would turn to crispy bacon. I wanted to fling myself on to the ground and worship them. Listen, nobody but the biggest and baddest man-on-road could walk around in those and, like, *live*?

First time I saw Dexter he was leaning against his BMW talking to Delmar. I could see he was checking me out, the new guy.

I used to dream Dexter was my brother. I imagined he lived in some massive Hollywood-style crib. I would arrive at the big gates and see a camera swivel as I approached. I would press the buzzer, be let in and would walk up a driveway that was a hundred yards long. A security guard would be waiting for me at the front door. He'd have a bald head and wear a black suit and black sunglasses, like in a Bond film. He'd say, 'The Chief is waiting for you, Mr Cole.'

*That's* what I'm talking about!

So Delmar was well protected and well respected. Girls loved him too. All the girls wanted a bad man. He got the best-looking ones. His girl Clarice looked like that Nicole from Pussycat Dolls. She lived in a detached house and everything. Delmar used to say she was so hot she was smoking. Delmar wouldn't go anywhere near the mingers on the estate.

So what was I gonna say to him and his crew? I didn't know so I just started talking. 'We, I mean *I*, got attacked,' I began, not sure whether to keep Adrian in the story. I didn't want Delmar to lump me together with someone who was a waste of space.

I told them about the Deptford Warriors. I said I'd been hit three times on the head with a baseball bat and said they could feel the bump that was still there. They laughed that off, though. Like it wasn't cool.

I didn't tell them who I was with or that we ran away before the madness kicked off.

The story just grew. I couldn't help myself. There were nearly forty of the Warriors, all with knives, broken bottles, baseball bats, and only ten of us. We tried to fight back but the Fedz arrived quickly and broke it up. One of the Fedz chased me but I escaped on to a railway track. Yeah, I exaggerated. Couldn't help it. The bull-shit took over.

They all gathered around and listened and I could tell from their faces they was well impressed. They'd heard about the fight, but didn't know anyone who was involved until then.

When I finished, Delmar lit up a cigarette and nodded his head like he thought I was cool. Well, maybe not cool, but not *not* cool, ya get me?

I noticed he stretched out his arm when he flicked the cigarette ash to protect those wicked Pradas.

Then his phone rang and he walked off to take a call. When he came back he said they had to be off but I should check them there later. They all got on their bikes and raced out.

Everyone knew you couldn't just join a gang for free unless you'd grown up in it. You had to prove yourself.

# Chapter Seven

# My Boy Adrian

I was relieved when I'd finally left the B-Block Boys way behind that afternoon and was nearly at the high street. Like I said, something was in the air. Someone was gonna lose their temper and I didn't want to be around when it happened. People always complained about the cold, but when it got hot they got nasty.

It was a busy Saturday afternoon and I could see the cars and people out shopping on the high street at the top of Redcross Street, in between the boarded-up houses. Not many people walked down Redcross, if they could help it, so it was nearly empty. It wasn't as bad as Murder Mile up the road. Still a kinda no-go area unless you lived there.

I only had my £5 pocket money so I was working out whether to get my Coke from the corner shop where they ripped you off, or walk all the way to Iceland, buy a budget box and take it home.

Big problem, though, no way did I want to go home, especially after you'd been stressing me out. You never bought me Coke, Mum. I used to beg you when I was a kid. You was always going on about me drinking water like it was a magic potion. I hated water. Why? 'Cos it had no taste, yeah? *Not* rocket science. I only drank it when I brushed my teeth and then spat it out again. Water mixed with Ribena, though? *Now* we're talking.

So I was dying of thirst as if I'd been lost in the desert for a week when I saw Adrian walking up ahead.

We hadn't talked for months. I usually nodded when I saw him but that was it. We'd never been in the same class at school so that wasn't a problem. I had my reputation to think of, all right?

Looking at him now I could really see how un-cool he was. For a start his baseball cap had a curved peak rather than a flat one. And, get this, his jeans hung down *under* his bum like it was 2008 and not 2009. Get wiv da program, Wimp-Boy. His jeans made him walk like a penguin and they kept falling down so he kept hitching them up.

Check this, Mum. Adrian had the kind of weak walk that said, 'Beat me up now!' Delmar had the kind of swagger that said, 'Back off or *you'll* get beat.' So who was I expected to roll with, huh?

I sent him a text. Couldn't help myself.

'Yo! Ade! Blud! Long time. Sorry I ain't been catching up wiv ya. Watch ur back. Fedz just knocked 4 u at my yard, innit. Said witnesses say u been dealing & dey iz looking 4 u.'

I saw him take his phone out of his pocket, read it, then start running towards the high street in a panic like he could hear sirens behind him already. His jeans kept falling down so's he couldn't run properly and he kept tripping up.

I cracked up at first. What jokes! What a mug! Then I felt a bit guilty so I ran to catch up with him.

'Oi! It's me!' I shouted when I caught up. 'I was joking you, Adrian. Ain't no Fedz on your tail.'

I couldn't believe it when I saw him wipe tears off his face. When was he gonna grow up? He was pleased to see me, though. Smiling with those stupid dimples and everything.

'And pull your jeans up properly. That low-slung look is so last year, man. And take that cap off, man. Honestly my boy, your style's all wrong without me to show you some certified swagger.'

He hitched up his jeans and tied the belt properly and took off his cap. Adrian was so obedient, man!

I punched him on his arm and he giggled and punched me back. I could tell he was grateful I was talking to him after so long.

'I see you're running with the Kamikaze Kru,' he said. I could see he was sorry we wasn't friends no more.

Then I thought about it. Adrian was always on his jacks, always walking on his own. Used to be the two of us. Maybe he was lonely?

'What did I do wrong, JJ?' He looked down, all embarrassed. I looked down too. That's when I saw he was wearing fricking sandals! Aw, please! What a hopeless case.

'You didn't do nothing wrong, Adrian. You just didn't do much right. You've got to step up and be a man. Life ain't no joke. Deptford was a bad scene and we was just lucky. I wanna live, you know, so I've gotta run with people who've got my back, y'understand?'

'I'll make sure I've got your back. I swear-down!' he squealed, like a little boy. I noticed his voice hadn't broken yet. I hadn't even noticed before! Mine had broken about a year ago.

Then he spun on his heel and back-skipped in front of me like we was back in primary school.

'Things will be different from now on,' he added.

'You've got to step up,' I said.

'I'll step up,' he repeated like a parrot.

I sort of knew he wouldn't but I liked him in spite of his childishness. I'd known him nearly all my life and he'd been my best friend. I kinda missed all the silly things we used to do.

'Wanna come round later?' I asked. 'My mum will be pleased to see you.'

This made him so happy I was sure he was gonna start crying again.

*Don't, my boy! Don't!*

'Oh. Course. I've got to be back by half-six, though!'

'Still on curfew then?'

'Yeah, yeah, but not for long.'

Then he went and ruined it all. Adrian suddenly got excited.

'Guess what, JJ. I've decided I'm going to be an architect.'

'What . . .? For what?'

Now what was he on about? Silliness again, for sure.

''Cos I like drawing and it's a good career. I'm going to take eight GSCEs, if they let me. I've got two years to get it together. I've worked really hard these past few months and came top of my classes in four subjects at the end of term. I got the Most Improved Student Award in my class. Mrs Mathison was well impressed. Me and her get on now. She thinks I could get straight A's if I work hard.

'Her husband is an architect in Hammersmith

and she said he'll take me on work placement next summer. I might even apply to university. Can you believe it? Mrs Mathison thinks I might have a chance. Dad's so pleased he's going to take out a loan and get me a computer and printer so I can work properly. He won't let me connect it to the internet yet, though.

'Trust me, I'm never coming back here. Not ever. I'm going to live away from all this street life. I've been dying to tell you. Your boy Adrian is a man with a plan!'

WTF! I was so gob-smacked I stopped in my tracks as if someone had slapped me in the face. Then the devil came out of me. I put my hand on his shoulder, took a deep breath, and said:

'Yo! Listen-up, you're aiming way too high, my boy. You're only fourteen. Who knows what will happen? You're not thinking straight. Get real. People like us don't leave this hood, yeah? We is gangsta, ya get me? And Ade, don't think you're better than me, 'cos you ain't.'

'But Mrs Mathison thinks I can do it!' he squeaked.

'Fuck Mrs Mathison!'

Yeah, yeah, tears were in his eyes again.

Me and Adrian stood at the top of Redcross. He was crying but trying to hide it by blowing his nose on his sleeve. I didn't want to hit him or nothing. Not this time. I just felt like a real bastard.

I didn't know what to do or say, so I looked up the high street and damn it! Delmar was standing right there, talking on his mobile. His eyes was running up and down Adrian like he was made of human turd. I was so embarrassed to be seen with Ade.

'Gotta go,' I said quickly. 'Catch ya later.' And I walked off.

I hoped Adrian wouldn't look after me. But when I turned around, he was watching me pumping fists with Delmar. Adrian looked crushed. Delmar looked suspicious.

'You still hanging with that candy ass?' he asked in the American accent he put on sometimes.

'Nah, nah,' I replied. 'I just bumped into him. Nah, nah, nah.'

'Is it?' he said, like he didn't believe me.

Then he said, 'You've got to keep a tight circle. You don't want too many people knowing you. You've got to protect your reputation, ya get me? So don't be hanging around with no candy ass.'

# Chapter Eight

# The High Street

It was so cool being seen with Delmar on the high street. Just the two of us this time, without the whole crew. It rubbed off on me. Most of the kids knew him from school. They all checked him. *Safe! Safe!*

Two cool dudes, ya get me? Brap-brap! (Respect!)

We went into the newsagent and Delmar bought four cans of Coke and gave two to me. I never asked or nothing. That's how he was, always giving me stuff, like my Rocawear jeans and Tupac T-shirt. Yeah, his cast-offs, but so what? I don't know why you objected. You should've been grateful someone was making me look decent.

He threw the coins for the Cokes on the counter and walked out without waiting for change. It was like he was telling the man to get stuffed. I wished I could do that but I would need my money, even if it was only 10p.

I knocked my Coke back in one go and so did he. Then we both burped at the same time and laughed. Well, I laughed. Delmar never really laughed properly. He was too cool for that. He kind of grunted with that sideways grin on his face. He crushed his can in one hand and threw it in the gutter. I didn't even try that one 'cos I'd just show myself up. So I chucked my can on the ground instead and kicked it.

Then this busted woman wearing high-heeled sandals stepped on it and nearly fell. Boy! Did she give me daggers. She opened her fat mouth to cuss me out. Then she saw Delmar. Ding dong! He just gave her one of his mean stares and kissed his teeth. She looked the other way and hurried past us.

That's how he was. Don't mess with The Delmar and don't mess with his crew too! SNM (Say no more!).

I hoped he would hang with me all afternoon and evening. What else was I gonna do? Sit in my room and slowly suffocate to death? Watch those boring history programmes you like? You know what I think of history, Mum. It's dead!

We walked down the high street and I noticed that Delmar walked in a straight line, like Tyrone. He wouldn't budge for no one. Not even women with prams. I tried doing the same as him but when I did, people just carried on walking like they was gonna knock me down and step right over me. One bloke looked like he was gonna head-butt me if I didn't move out the way. So while Delmar walked in a straight line like he owned the place, I had to skip around, like I didn't.

We'd probably hook up with the rest of the Kamikaze Kru later. But I didn't care. So long as I rolled with him, life was way too good, ya get me?

The high street was safe ground for all the local crews during the day. At night it was a no man's land – deserted, most of the shops locked up behind metal shutters.

Delmar and the crew sometimes went down it at night, but only on their bikes. Not me, of course. Why? Obvious! I didn't have a bike, innit, although Delmar said he'd give me his BMX Slammer soon, 'cos he was going to have one customized for him.

When they all cycled off, I stayed behind at the estate and waited for them to come back. They never really told me what they got up to but I reckoned it was because I was the new boy. Delmar told me they just cycled round the park. So how come they came back with chips from the high street sometimes? I wasn't stupid. As I had private detective skills, I knew they was up to something. It did make me feel left out. Like I didn't really belong properly yet.

Most nights I dreamt of having my own BMX. You know that bit at the end of *ET* when those boys start flying through the air on their bikes? I'd only started having that dream. Me cycling my BMX down the high street and everyone chasing me – the B-Block Boys, the Deptford Warriors, the Camberwell Campaign, the Fedz, newsagent, bus drivers, Delmar and the Kamikaze Kru, yeah, even you. Not Shontelle, though. Then all of a sudden, just when everyone's nearly catching up with me, my bike takes off like it's got wings and I'm flying through the air towards the moon.

Mum, that was the best dream ever. It made me feel really happy.

Me and Delmar sat down on a wall outside the Texaco gas station, which was in the shade under a big tree. The only fricking tree on the high street. Usually drunks and tramps sat on that wall but it was empty.

We just watched everyone. Opposite was Iceland, next to it the job centre, Las Vegas Nails, Ladbrokes Bookmakers, Huang-Nam Supermarket, launderette, USA Nails, the One Pound Shop, Elegance Hair & Beauty, Queenie's Jerk City.

Further down there was William Hill Bookmakers, Pringles Bakery, Superdrug, Cheap Flights

– but not cheap enough, eh? I hated going back to school in September 'cos kids was always bragging about where they'd been. Margate, Devon, Disneyland Paris, Spain, Greece, Caribbean, Turkey, Poland, Albania, all these African and Arab and easterly-type places. I told myself one day I was gonna go on holiday, too. I knew you couldn't afford it so I never went on about it. But I used to have this fantasy that I'd go back to school after the summer holidays and tell everyone I'd been somewhere, just anywhere. Even Margate. Just somewhere!

Even Adrian had been to Ghana three times.

Delmar lit up a cigarette and was blowing smoke rings. He offered me one but I said no. I'd only ever had, like, ten cigarettes in my life, and I wasn't going to smoke anywhere you could see me and give me a hard time after.

'I've never been on a plane,' I said. 'What's it like?'

Last Christmas Delmar had visited his uncle who lived in Brooklyn in New York.

'Awwww man!' he replied, in his thick American accent. 'You ain't lived, Buddy, until you've been up in dem skies so high like a fly! You ain't lived until you've flown first class and you've got 7,000 films to choose from and fifty music channels. You ain't lived, JJ, until you've flown into JFK airport at night and seen dem lights all a-bright and a-shiny below. You ain't lived, JJ, until you've driven through the means streets of Brooklyn and seen gangstas in da hood shootin' each other up!'

Delmar was born and raised in, like, Tottenham? Every time he went fake American I felt like giggling. One time I copied him and spoke in American too. I thought Delmar would think it was fun. No way! He looked like he was ready to bitch-slap me. So I stopped. He was a cool dude, though.

So we was on the wall chatting nonsense when I looked over at Iceland and I couldn't believe my fricking eyes! Keith was coming out with some woman and a little boy who was about the same age as Shontelle, right? I see he's carrying loads of bags and holding the boy's hand like he's a proper father. It makes me think how Shontelle has never even seen him.

I couldn't believe it. I hadn't seen that bastard for about three years. And check this now, he crosses the road and starts walking in my direction, not seeing me. And my bum is like stuck to the wall as if it has been welded on to it. I want to run but I can't. I know our eyes are gonna lock soon and then – WTF!

Delmar didn't notice a thing. He's going on being American and telling me about how he hung out with Jay-Z and Beyoncé last Christmas. It was at his, like, cousin's friend's brother's uncle's party in Brooklyn or something? I know I was supposed to be well impressed but, well, he was bullshitting me, right? Well, maybe. I wasn't sure 'cos Delmar wasn't like anyone else I knew. I mean, his cool factor went through the roof.

So there was Keith. There was me. And time stopped. Just like in that telly programme *Heroes* where everything freezes.

Whenever I look at Shontelle I think of Keith. I know she's our cutie pie and everything but I can't help it. She looks just like him. Light skin, loose hair, slanty eyes.

I couldn't believe it when you gave him a key to our flat. As soon as you heard him turning it in the front door you sent me to my bedroom, even though we was in the middle of watching *CSI Miami* or something. You'd act different around him, too, as if everything he said was clever and funny. One minute you'd be having a go at me and the next you'd be licking his boots.

I know he beat you. 'Course I did. I heard you begging him to stop even though you tried to keep quiet. I'd sit on my bed cuddling Barnaby the One-Eyed Bandit and listening for any sounds he was hurting you.

Even when you was pregnant with Shontelle

he gave you enough licks. I used to dream he'd die suddenly, have a heart attack or something, or get stabbed up by an enemy. I was sure everyone must hate him except you.

I didn't even dare creep across the hall carpet to the bog in case he came out and got me too. Remember how I used to wet my bed in those days and you was furious? Well, now you know why.

All night I'd stay awake thinking you was lying on the floor in a pool of blood like in *CSI*. In the morning I'd hear him open the door quietly like a robber.

Now, this is what really got me. I'd walk into the kitchen and you'd be eating Kellogg's in your dressing-gown as if nothing had happened. You was acting like you was in a cereal advert on telly. All happy-happy and smiling. 'Morning, Jerome. Shall I make you some toast or I can do you a fried breakfast today?'

Like I was so stupid? Like I didn't know what was going on?

One morning I told you I hated him. 'Please accept him, Jerome. I love him so much.' Yeah, that's what you said. That meant you loved him more than me.

After Shontelle was born, he stopped coming round. I saw how you was always looking up at sounds near the front door as if hoping he was coming back. You didn't even dump him. He dumped you. Shame!

I never told you this, either, but one time, after the pubs had closed, he passed me and Adrian on the stairs having a puff of weed that Adrian had stolen from his older brother. Keith had the cheek to tell me off when I know he sat in our sitting room with you smoking weed like a zombie. I could smell it.

Well, I just blew smoke in his face, didn't I. Why? 'Cos I felt like it. He wasn't my dad last time I looked! What did he do? He picked me up by my jacket, punched me twice in the stomach with his great big fist, and threw me down the stairs. Nearly broke my fricking neck!

I was bawling but he just said, 'Keep your damn mouth shut!' But quietly, so no one would come out of their flats and see what was going on.

How old was I? Ten years old, Mum. Ten years old!

I tell you, if I was in the Kamikaze Kru then, he wouldn't have dared. Or if he did, they would have got him and got him good.

Let me tell you something else, too. Devon, who is in my crew, is one of his kids. I never told you that. So he's Shontelle's half-brother. Looks a bit like her too. The eyes and loose hair. Devon said Keith has kids all over the place. A whole bag of baby-mothers, ya get me?

So how could you choose someone like him? Then I thought, maybe that's why you stopped having boyfriends after Shontelle was born. Maybe you'd had enough.

As for my dad. I last saw him when I was six, yeah? The number of times I waited for him to turn up when he'd promised to take me to McDonald's or see a film. You remember I'd wait in the sitting room in my best clothes. Barnaby the One-Eyed Bandit was dressed up in his best clothes, too. I'd sit there for hours waiting for the bell to ring. The last time it was Easter and he'd promised me a big Easter egg. I was so excited, wasn't I, Mum? You told me to calm down 'cos I was jumping around the room and running to the door every few minutes. I waited hours. No show.

The sky outside got darker and so did the room. You was slamming doors and stuff. Hey, maybe I learnt that from you! (LOL!) You told me to get ready for bed. That's when I knew he wasn't coming for me.

You used to say, 'Your father and I loved each other very much, Jerome, but it didn't work out.'

So tell me, Mum. How long did you love each other for? A week? A month? A year? Two years?

50

Not long enough to be a proper family. You was always going on about me using condoms but what about you? You chose the bad guys. That's the truth.

Keith had now crossed the road and I was sitting right in front of the bastard. He didn't recognize me at first 'cos I was so tall and not baby-faced no more. Then he stopped and did a double-take.

His woman looked at him and then at me and you know what? She thought I was one of his kids. She *did*! It was in her eyes, like, a bit shocked, a bit angry, a bit jealous.

I saw his eyes glaze over the way our teachers do when they see us in the school corridors or on the streets. Then he carried on walking and she ran her eyes up and down me like *I* was the scumbag and followed him.

I watched them walk down the high street like a normal family. She was wearing one of those tops that tied at the neck. Brown it was and you could see all her shiny flabby back. A tight brown skirt, too, that showed her lumps. Mum, she was so minging. Her heels was so high she walked forwards like she was gonna fall flat on her face any minute.

I hoped she would.

You was better than that. You dressed nicely.

Respectable. I'll say that for you. You was always going on about being ugly but you wasn't, not really. You just looked ordinary. Anyway, if you was ugly how could you produce a handsome son like me! (LMAO!)

I watched Keith disappear into the crowds.

If someone had put a diamond-studded, gold-plated semi-automatic pistol in my hands, I'd have taken him out in one.

Yeah, I would, Mum. *Believe!*

# Chapter Nine

# School of Life

Delmar got a text, jumped down from the wall and stamped out his cigarette end.

'I'm bored,' he said. 'Let's rock over to Dexter's.'

Those were the magic words I'd been waiting to hear ever since I started hanging with him. I wanted to meet the man who ran this hood, ya get me? Dexter was King. He was the Main Man. The Mash Man. The Big Daddy. He was Da Don.

We began to walk again. The air was so heavy it was like the sky was falling down on us and covering us in a blanket. The crowds was so thick everyone became a blur of faces and voices. It was like being at Oxford Circus last Christmas Eve when you let me go to Nike Town to get your present for me – my first pair of Nike trainers! Brap! Brap!

Cars was honking their horns and rubbish music coming out of the rubbish shops. Some people smelt rank too, yeah? Like they had a curry and beer the night before and didn't know what soap and Sure Maximum Protection Deodorant was. There's me walking along and some tall bloke in a vest scratches his head and almost puts his wet, hairy armpit in my face. I thought I was gonna pass out with the fumes, man. Stinking up the place. Pure badness!

Even Delmar couldn't walk in a straight line no more. Everyone was bumping everyone as well, worse than usual. It was like playing dodg-ems. Delmar had gone quiet, like he was thinking. I didn't like it when he went quiet. I thought I'd done something wrong. So I started talking about that rapper called Chipmunk who's only eighteen. I mean he's good, like, but way too cocky, way too cocky. I know you've never heard of him, old lady! Don't pretend you have.

Silence.

So then I started going on about whether the beef between 50 Cent and The Game was really over like it says in The Game's song, 'Better on the Other Side'. 'Cos Michael Jackson tried to stop their beef, and now he's dead they're supposed to be cool with each other. And I was saying how if those guys wasn't careful they'd end up like Tupac and Biggie Smalls. D-E-A-D.

Some wicked lyrics came to me: *Six feet under/*

*And ya gonna miss yo mama/ 'Cos ya didn't turn the other cheek/ 'Cos ya didn't want to be seen as weak.*

That's when Delmar punched his fist in his palm and spat out, 'Squash it, JJ!'

It was like he wanted to punch me. I knew Delmar was well-hard, Mum, but he'd never shouted at me before. I hadn't done nothing, yeah? He was the worst bumper, too, even with grown-up men who looked harder than him. Like he was angry no one in the crowd was respecting him no more. If some big mandem decided to teach him a lesson then everything would go nuts. If that happened, I wasn't gonna stay around. No way.

That's when I realized, me and Adrian was the same, innit?

I was so relieved when we'd moved through the stinking crowds and left the top end of the high street behind and was walking towards my school.

There it was, on the opposite side of the road, the sign: William Holland School. Comprehensive. Headmistress. Dr Margaret Anderson. Founded 1912.

Funny, but I'd never really looked at that sign before. It was just there. I mean I had other things on my mind when I walked into school. I had to be on my guard. It was like going to that Afghanistan-place in Africa. War. Ya get me?

School looked like a mental asylum when it was so deserted. Serious! A big ugly old building built in the days when kids didn't have shoes and people was dying from the plague and Queen Victoria was on the throne and the Nazis was bombing us. A bit before your time, then, Mumsy. Just a bit. (LMAO!)

These were the rules of the mental asylum.

For a start, don't bring your mobile phone to school or someone will take it off you.

Two, don't ride your bike to school, 'cos someone will use chain-cutters on it.

Three, don't wear platinum, gold or even silver jewellery unless you've got a bruv called The Dexter!

Four, don't carry more than £2 and if you do, hide it in your briefs (not socks 'cos they'll make you take off your shoes).

Five, don't look at anyone you don't know, 'cos they might stab you up for disrespecting them.

Six, don't bring a knife into school 'cos they'll search your bag at the entrance. Throw it over the wall instead and pick it up later, yeah?

Seven, don't take drugs, just sell them.

Eight, if you're gonna bring in a replica gun, don't wave it around at assembly 'cos you'll end up being excluded.

Nine, join a gang for protection.

Ten, if you can avoid all of the above, get educated. Boring!

The only teacher I liked was Mr Akintayo who took us for Maths. It's not like the rest were all bad but he was the only one we respected, even though Maths was invented to torture schoolchildren. The first day he walked into the classroom he just stood there looking at us until we shut up.

He said, 'If you behave, I'll behave. If you don't, I won't.' And that's how it played.

He'd say, 'Shut up and listen,' and if you didn't, he'd give you detention. No second chance or nothing. You did the littlest thing like make jokes out loud, or backchat him, and you got detention or sent to the Head. I tell you, that man didn't mess. You know I got enough detentions my first term with him.

After a while I stopped mucking about at the back and it was like he began to respect me. He was always getting me to answer questions instead of picking the class creeps who always put their hands up first. If my homework was crap he'd sit on my desk and say, 'Jerome, you know you can do better than that. For yourself, for your family, for your community.' It made me want to work harder. He never gave me that look teachers have, like they'd rather fry their eyeballs than be in the same room as you.

The other teachers were pussies, like Miss Dixon. Her voice used to shake when she took us for English. She was always wiping sweat off her top lip too. And she'd put her handbag in the desk and lock it, even though she never left the classroom.

Mr Akintayo wasn't afraid of us, even though some of us was way bigger than him. He was on our side.

Me and Delmar passed Mohammad's Fish and Chips at the corner. Best smell in the world! You know it! Fish and chips with vinegar wrapped in paper. I really hoped Delmar would crack his face and smile. We could get some chips later and have a laugh. The shop was open but empty. During the week it was crammed with kids. Especially my boy Ade, who ate chips nearly every day after school. Then he'd go home to his mum's cooking. The men who worked there hated us. Like I said, everyone did.

Once we'd passed school Delmar began to talk to me again, although I could tell he was still a bit annoyed.

'I hate living in this shit-hole. I deserve better.

Soon as I can I'm going to move to Miami and live on Romeo Drive or Rodeo Drive or something. See me now cruising down the highway in my Hummer with two fit bitches in the back. I'll come back and visit Mum, Delice and Dexter but that's it. Not *him*. My dad can rot in prison, far as I'm concerned. He should've been more careful, ya get me? As Mum says, only a dad can turn you into a man, innit? Instead I've spent my whole life being dragged into prison to see him. Once a month and I've always hated it. No more! I've told Mum. I'm not going into sixth form, either. What's the point when people like us don't get good jobs. I can make plenty dollar anyhow.'

Then he turned and looked at me funny, like he was waiting for me to ask a question. So I did and said, 'What's anyhow?'

I kinda knew really.

'I do stuff for Dexter, you know?'

'What stuff?'

'Don't act all innocent, JJ. What d'ya think?'

Of course I knew, Mum. I'd always known what the Kamikaze Kru was up to but I didn't want to think about it.

'Dexter says it's time to bring you in. You ready?'

I was almost going to ask, 'Bring me in to what?' but I knew he'd get mad at me.

'I like you, JJ,' he said. 'You're pretty safe these days.'

I wanted to jump up and punch the air. Raaaah! At last someone thought I was COOL!!! And not just anyone but The Delmar! He liked me too! Instead I just, like, nodded, the way he nodded at most things. A kind of – yeah, whatever, I'm too cool for school – kinda nod.

'So this is how it goes,' he went on. 'When we get there, be nice to him but don't, like, grovel, 'cos Dexter don't like grovellers, ya get me?'

I said, 'Aye, aye, sir,' and saluted like I was in the army.

Delmar slid his eyes over to me. 'Cut it out, JJ. Don't act like a kid when you're there, either, or he'll throw you out.'

I kept forgetting I was, like, cool.

'So look now,' he continued. 'Dexter has his own thing going on but he wants to spread his wings and move into NW15, which as you know is run by the B-Block Boys and their Olders. They're useless, though, and most of the Olders are inside for dealing and the Youngers are wankers, as we know. Dexter's got some customers lined up. Don't worry, my man. It's down by the station so it's the other side of Brampton Estate so you'll be safe, all right? You won't be bumping into the B-Block twats when you're there. Dexter needs more runners 'cos he's expanding his business empire, ya get me? He's dealing direct now with the top man in Liverpool. Check this, the Liverpool man deals *direct* with the Colombians.'

Colombians? Colombians! C-O-L-O-M-B-I-A-N-S!

Delmar paused for his words to sink in. All of a sudden it was like I was in *Scarface* and rolling with the drug barons.

'Four packages, four flats. You'll be on trial, right? Are you on or are you on, my man?'

Like, I didn't see how I could say no. Delmar was my friend, right? What else was I gonna do? He didn't say what was in the packages. And it wasn't stealing, Mum. It's not, like, I was grabbing someone's mobile phone or handbag or anything.

He made my mind up for me.

'There's fifty quid in it for you. More if you prove yourself.'

What?! That was, like, ten weeks' pocket money! Was he kidding?

I broke into a smile in spite of trying to stay cool. I wanted to do that back skip that Adrian had done earlier. I was on a mega-buzz.

'Yeah, but watch it,' he added. 'Once you're stuck in the game, that's it.'

Delmar lit up another fag and inhaled so much

of it I thought he was gonna burn down the whole fag in one go. It was a big-man thing to do. Like he was thinking deep thoughts.

When he blew the smoke out, it came down his nose.

'That's nothing, bruv,' he said. 'I get £350 a week, easy. Don't even have to sort out my mum 'cos Dexter looks after her. You know my flat is the most luxurious on the estate. You *know* it. Real wooden floors, not that imitation stuff everyone else has, shag-pile carpets, top-range dishwasher. You know our white leather sofa? Cost £3,000. That's why Mum's covered it in plastic. You know that life-sized china panther in the sitting room with the ashtray built into its head? Cost £1,400, my man. Anything Mum wants, she asks Dexter. He keeps most of my money in the bank for me 'cos I'm saving for my first Hummer.'

'Yeah, cool, bruv,' I replied.

This wasn't for real. Was it? Could I have a Hummer too? It was like all of a sudden all my dreams was possible. I could touch them like they was real. Yeah, it was like touching them.

I was already thinking how if I was earning big money I could get Shontelle a proper fifth birthday present. Like one of those talking dolls she's always going on about and some pretty dresses from Mothercare instead of Primark. And how I could take you shopping in Sainsbury's instead of Iceland. Whatever you want, Mum. Whatever you want. Jerome was gonna be the Man of the House, ya get me?

# Chapter Ten

# Dexter's Yard

We'd begun walking up the hill to where there wasn't no more estates. All the people from the high street seemed to have disappeared. It was like there was a rope dividing the two areas and no one went beyond it. Up there all the buildings were low and everyone lived in houses. Not mansions like Blackheath Common, because those houses was so big it was ridiculous.

I was so excited when we turned off the main road. I said to myself – this is *it*! This is *it*!

Except it wasn't, really. Mayflower Close? Didn't sound like no gangsta's hood. It was a dead-end street with new Brookside-type houses. They had small lawns with no fences around them like in American films. Nah, surely Dexter didn't live in this boring-nothing place, right? I expected one of those flash footballer cribs you was always looking at in *Hello* magazine.

Delmar knocked on the door of No. 51. It looked

like every other house there except the front door didn't have a glass window in it, just wood.

Dexter's BMW was parked up outside. Black, shiny, beau-ti-ful!

Some bloke answered the door. Mum, imagine four of me rolled into one person, yeah? Well, that's how big this dude was. No lie! I bet he had to walk sidewards to get in the door. He pumped fists with Delmar and I hoped he wouldn't do it with me or I'd go flying back into the street. He let us in and then he disappeared upstairs, the steps creaking.

We walked through to the kitchen at the back and there was The Dext! He had his Kanye West LV Don trainers up on the table and was stroking this grey and white dog. Mum, I know you like dogs but it was the fugliest one I've ever seen. It looked like a cross between a staff bull and a pit bull and it looked like someone had bashed its face in with a hammer. It was dribbling all over the place too, like one of those inbred fighting dogs.

Guess what Dexter said to me? 'Lucy here will rip out your throat if I tell her to.'

I nearly wet my pants. No lie!

He gave me a funny look, like he would do it too. Kind of staring so that his eyes burned holes in me. It was the same look Delmar had sometimes. Yeah, it was exactly the same!

65

'Sit, sit!' he said, and me and Delmar sat down at the table. It was covered with crumbs and ash and even dog's hairs. The sink was piled up with takeaway packets and all kinds of crap was coming out of the bin. You'd go ballistic. Running around with a pan and brush and bleach.

I'd never seen Dexter close up before. Delmar was fifteen but looked older. Dexter was nineteen but looked his age. So they both kinda looked the same age. Close up I could see that mega-chain around Dexter's neck had a big pendant that said 'DEATHROW RECORDS'. And I saw his ring. Raaaah! It was so cool. It was three gold rings on three fingers with one gold band across it that said 'THUGLOVE'.

Dexter's baseball cap had a curved peak. Damn! Styles was always changing so fast. I had to tell Ade. Dexter had dark brown patches on his face and his teeth stuck out. Mandem needed braces. Even so, he had a gold tooth with a diamond inside it.

Then Dexter threw the dog off his lap and I hoped it wouldn't jump up at me. I didn't want that manky thing nowhere near me. Yuk! Dexter leaned his elbows on the table like he was about to say something important. I felt dirty just sitting in that kitchen.

'Look here, JJ. Everything will be cool if you

just follow the rules. See what I have here? Nice house and everything and I ain't even twenty yet. You too, blud. You too. In time all this will be yours. Seen?'

He waved his arm around the kitchen like he was Marlon Brando in *The Godfather* and we was sitting in some mansion looking out on to hundreds of miles of estate with lawns and a lake and everything. I thought, I hope not, Blud. I hope not. (LOL!)

'Keep your mouth shut about whatever you do for me. I don't care if the Fedz catch you. We've never met. Don't even think of snaking on me. Even if I was in prison, I control these roads. Unnerstan'?'

I nodded my head, hoping he could see I could be trusted.

Then he said, 'You've got a mum and cute little sister Shontelle, right?' He eyeballed me again.

Mum, I was so shocked. Then I looked over at Delmar who looked away. WTF!

'Next up, once you're in, you're in. So you have a choice right now, JJ. You can just walk out that door and everything is cool. Or you can stay, but if you stay, you're repping me. Do you feel me, JJ?'

'I feel you, Dexter.'

'Are you in, JJ?'

'Sure I am!'

The words came out before I even thought them.

You know how I said I was just angry after Deptford, with my head all foggy and stuff. Well, it was like I'd just been slapped in the face and was waking up. What had I got myself into?

Then he pulled this brown rucksack out from under his chair, opened it up, and took out a pistol and laid it on the table.

OMG! (Oh my God!) I'd never seen a gun before. I'd never even seen a replica before. I knew it was a pistol. It wasn't gold-plated, neither, but it was black and the handle was made of wood. It looked heavy.

I couldn't believe what I was seeing. I didn't even want to pick it up. It just looked, so, like, *deadly.*

'This weapon here can kill a man,' Dexter said, eyeballing me. It was like he was warning me.

Mum, I wanted to run out of that house and back down the hill. But what would I say to Delmar afterwards? He'd have nothing to do with me and then I'd be on my jacks. Or just me and Adrian again. No protection. No nothing. All I wanted was to make some money and stay safe, Mum. But I felt like I was already stuck in too deep.

Dexter gave me this twisted grin, but I didn't feel like smiling back. He told Delmar to take me into the sitting room while he sorted stuff out.

The sitting room was two small rooms knocked into one. The curtains was closed and it stank of stale smoke and sweat. Didn't nobody open any windows in that place? Didn't nobody know it was so hot outside everyone was breathing like they had asthma?

The first half of the room had a big white leather sofa and armchairs, all covered in plastic. There was a blue carpet, a low table and a sideboard with Bose speakers. In the back half of the room there was a pool table, which was pretty cool.

I remember thinking how you, me and Shontelle could really spread out in a pad like this.

I know what you're thinking? Yep! There was a 50-inch plasma telly. Am-az-ing! The kind that costs thousands of pounds. I'd never seen one so big in real life.

Delmar sat down and put the telly on. I just stood and when he told me to sit, I ignored him. He just shrugged and said, 'You'll get my BMX soon, anyway.'

Then he started zapping between channels. Sky – hundreds of them.

A bit later Dexter came in with four packages, really small, like the size of teabags. They fitted in my pocket easy. He gave me the addresses on a piece of paper and told me to meet Delmar inside the chip shop near my school once I'd done the delivery.

That's when he put the flick knife in my hand. It had a black handle and was about six inches long. WTF!

'You can keep it. I have plenty more,' he said, laughing.

'Nah, nah, I don't need it,' I said, backing away from it. But Dexter took my hand, opened my palm, slapped the knife into it, closed my fingers over it and squeezed my fist so hard I almost yelped like a puppy dog when you've stepped on its feet.

'You'll be thanking me if you need to use it. Unnerstan'?'

This was some heavy shit, yeah? Before I could say anything else he almost pushed me towards the door.

'All right, soldier?' he said, slapping me on the back.

'Yeah, cool.'

# Final Chapter

# The Chip Shop

Once I'd left Dexter's I felt my cheeks get wet. Couldn't help it. Me, *the* JJ, crying like a kid. I was so relieved to be out of that stuffy place, though. I wanted to come home and scrub its nastiness off me in the shower. I was thinking about how you was cooking garlic and onions before I left the flat. That meant a curry, I reckon. Goat? Mutton? Chicken? You always cooked it Saturday and let it marinate overnight for Sunday dinner. I was thinking how much I liked your food, Mum. You was the best cook in the world. Even when you made mashed potato it wasn't like that boring stuff they gave you at school. You mixed it with herbs and spices and cheese and cream and fried cabbage with fried onions and carrots. Wick-ed! Ya get what I'm saying? Off the hook, Mumsy. Off – the – hook!

It was cooler outside. I checked the time – 5.45 p.m. I reckoned it would take me about twenty-five minutes to do the job and get back to the chip shop.

Big problem, though. I didn't want to do the job, or did I?

I had all these voices in my head shouting at the same time. Yours was telling me to stay out of trouble. Adrian was telling me he was a man with a plan. Delmar was telling me I was now cool. Dexter was telling me his fugly dog could rip out my throat. Even Mr Akintayo came into my head, telling me I could do better.

As I walked down the hill I kept seeing Dexter's gun on the table. It looked so innocent, just metal and wood, but those things killed people, Mum. They did! It was like I was just realizing. That's *murder*. That means someone *dies*. Someone like you or Shontelle or Adrian. In America they'd put you in the electric chair in some places and electrify you.

This wasn't no game. This wasn't no film or telly programme or rap video. This was the real thing.

You know how I said that after Deptford my head was all foggy and I couldn't think clearly? Well, as I walked down the hill to the high street the fog kinda lifted and my head got clear.

All your voices got quieter and just drifted away. Then I heard my own voice telling me I had to do what I had to do, like Tony Montana.

It would all be all right.

Was I scared? Too right I was. I was scared the Fedz might stop-and-search me again. They never found nothing before. I was scared as well that the B-Block Boys would see me slipping into their end and rush me.

Mum, I can hear you saying, 'Why didn't you come to me?' Like I could? Like you could do anything anyway? Like you wouldn't give me even more of a hard time than usual?

The high street was still busy but quieter as a lot of the shops was closing. This time I walked near the kerb, stepping on to the road to avoid people, even though the cars and buses could run me over. There were a few misses! In a way I was tempting it – like saying, take me now! Get it over with.

The knife felt really heavy in my pocket, even though it wasn't. I thought maybe people knew what I was doing. Maybe they could read my mind. What if I'm mugged and the gear is robbed? Would Dexter believe me?

I passed Redcross Street but walked further on and down towards the station to the other side of Brampton Estate. I began to feel like a big rock was in my stomach. Brampton Road was busy 'cos of the train station. All kinds of people was walking up and down it.

Women carrying shopping bags with little kids hanging on to the bags. Like you and Shontelle.

Those rich people, too, who you said moved into the area after the riots 'cos the rents was cheap and they wanted to slum it. Blonde Sienna Miller girls with denim shorts and loud, posh voices. Thin boys with floppy, greasy fringes covering most of their spotty faces and jeans so skinny their legs looked like black pencils.

Groups of wannabe Beyoncés looking more like the Sugababes on a bad-hair day, ya get me? Walking along wearing Primark Fashion and cutting their eyes at me like I'm interested and they're not. Whatever, man. KMT! (Kiss my teeth!)

Geriatrics hobbling down the hill. I tell you, I steered well clear of them and their walking sticks!

People who looked like they worked on the high street and wore dark suits but who caught the train out of Hellsville in the evening.

As soon as I saw Brampton Estate up ahead I stopped, slipped just inside the train station and scoped the entrance like I was Matt Damon in *The Bourne Identity*. There was loads of little kids hanging around, and a few bigger ones too. I tried to see if any of them was from the B-Block Boys but I couldn't see none I recognized.

I knew I had to go through them to get into the estate. Instead I was thinking – look, JJ, you could just jump on a train and, like, run away or something.

You know what, though, Mum? Man have fe do what man have fe do. So I began walking towards them keeping my head down like I was invisible. Then I hid behind this really big bloke. But he suddenly crossed the road without warning, leaving me all exposed and everything! Thanks! I was sure they was all gonna stop when they saw me and go silent. But they was just little kids, yeah? So they ignored me.

I found the right flats in the middle of the estate. I remember thinking how they wasn't near the entrance, like Delmar said. He was a liar! I kept looking around to check I wasn't being watched. Then I heard someone talking behind me and when I looked behind me saw someone turn a corner. I nearly died. I swear down! But it was just this geriatric with lots of Iceland shopping bags muttering to himself, like they do. He didn't even notice me. Then I saw three older boys race past on the other side of one of the arches and I just, like, froze and couldn't move. The last one was slower and looked at me but he didn't stop or nothing so I was sure he didn't really check me.

As for the job – four flats in the same building. I climbed the stairs, rang the bells of the flats, handed the packages over to the people who answered. Two men who looked like scummy crack-heads, one older woman who didn't, and the last one a girl about Shontelle's age who said her dad was still in bed.

I tell you, Mum. It was so easy I did smile to myself. *Not* rocket science. LOL! I could get a Hummer just by being a postman!

As soon as I'd dropped off the last package I wanted to run out of that place until I was back on Brampton Road. I remember thinking, what if word's got round and the B-Block Boys are waiting for me where those kids was hanging? I remember standing outside the last flat and peering over the balcony to see if anything was going on down below. Nothing. It was, like, empty, which was a bit spooky, too. I remember thinking – I got in but can I get out?

Mum, I crept down those concrete stairs like they was made of wood and creaked and someone underneath would hear me. When I reached the bottom it was like my eyes became two ping-pong balls spinning in every direction looking for signs of danger. But there was nothing. I began to walk quickly out of the estate but tried to look casual.

Just before I got to the entrance again, I hid behind a wall and scoped it. Nothing. Nobody.

Like, in a few minutes all the kids had gone off, yeah? I bet their mums had called them in for tea. I was well relieved. I almost started to run but I stopped myself.

When I got on to Brampton Road I thought – job done, my man. JOB DONE. Yeah, all in a day's work. And say hello to fifty large ones and some fish and chips and more ketchup than *you'd* say was good for me. 'It'll give you a sugar rush, Jerome.' Oh please, like I was still five or something.

I did almost run up the high street, which was getting emptier by the second. It was like that, once the shops was closed no one wanted to hang around. No one wanted to be the last person walking down an empty street. Even the McDonald's, KFC and takeaways closed early.

The shops were pulling down their shutters and I could hear the sound of alarms beeping as they was being set.

When I passed the wall at the Texaco station, I thought of Keith. I'd forgotten all about him. I was thinking that I'd tell you I saw him, but I'd miss out the bit about the busted woman he was with and the boy who looked the same age as Shontelle.

Finally, I got to the chip shop. I looked over at my school and thought maybe I should be like Delmar and leave at sixteen. What was the point?

Delmar was in the chip shop eating cod and chips. He could have waited, yeah? The men behind the counter looked me up and down when I walked in as if to see if I was trouble. They decided I wasn't so they turned away.

I sat down opposite Delmar, who was sitting in a back corner. He had ketchup dripping on his chin. I didn't tell him.

'Deed done, my man?' he asked me with his mouth open and full of chips. No table manners. I hadn't noticed before.

'Deed done, bruv,' I replied, thinking he wasn't my bruv. No way.

'Good. Have some chips and whatever else,' he said, and threw a fiver over at me.

I didn't want to pick it up but I did anyway.

This is how it kicked off.

I walked over to the counter and ordered haddock, chips and mushy peas, a Coke and six sachets of ketchup.

I heard some noise at the door and looked over and saw some boys riding up on their bikes, about four of them.

I realized they was the B-Block Boys but as soon as I did, they ran into the shop and dragged me out with them.

I shouted 'Delmar! Delmar!' as they jostled me, telling me they was gonna teach me a lesson for being where I shouldn't be.

I knew I was in for a beating. I knew Delmar would come out. He was big enough to help me. Or the chip shop men, but no one showed. When I looked over I saw the chip shop men had shut the door and one of them was on the phone.

I could see cars going past, slowing down but not stopping.

The gang crowded me and began pushing and punching me. They was cussing and telling me I was gonna get it. They weren't playing, neither. I remembered the flick knife but I was afraid to take it out. I didn't want to stab no one, Mum.

I'd never been beaten up before. It hurts like mad, you know. I thought they'd stop, but they didn't so I pulled out the knife and flicked it open. My hand was shaking so bad. I made some stupid jabs and cut someone's arm before two of them held my arm and made the knife drop. Then they all pushed me to the ground and started kicking and punching me. They was kicking me in the face as if I was a football. They was kicking me in my ribs so that I'm sure I felt some of them crack. They kicked me in my balls which was the worst pain of all.

I could feel my mouth fill with blood and my teeth come loose and everywhere hurt. I tried to curl up into a ball but they wouldn't let me. They stretched out my legs and arms and just laid into me. They was a bit older than me, and well-hard. I kept expecting Delmar to show or someone else to come to my rescue. For the first time in my life I wanted to see a policeman show up, yeah.

My head began to feel like that mutton curry you was probably cooking right at that moment. Like it was going soft inside. My eyes was blurry too.

That's when I saw Tyrone. He must have held back. He looked even more scary than he normally did. You could tell Tyrone hated the whole world. I remember thinking how I'd hate to be his mum. He wasn't human.

He just said, 'You've got to be taught a lesson. You've got to learn respect.'

He had a knife. Just like a carving knife from the kitchen. Like the one you got from Argos except it had a red handle instead of a yellow one. I saw the knife come towards me but I didn't feel nothing at first.

Then my eyes closed. Remember you used to say that giving birth was the worst pain in the world? Trust me, it's not.

The last thing I felt was the knife going into my neck.

That's when my heart went cold.

Then I saw them all standing above me but I knew I was dead. My eyes was open and my mouth was bleeding but I knew I was dead. Then they disappeared.

Everything faded until I couldn't see nothing no more. I couldn't feel nothing no more.

The worst bit was knowing you'd be upset. I know I annoyed you like hell and you annoyed me like hell but I was still your son and you was still my mum.

That's why I wanted to write you this letter. You needed to know why your son died. You needed to know everything I never told you.

I wanted you to know I hadn't been mixed up in badness for a long time – just for twenty-five minutes of my fourteen years of life.

So now you know, I can say goodbye.

Jerome Cole-Wallace
1995–2009

# Acknowledgements

Thanks to Juliette Mitchell, my editor on this book, and to the teams at Hamish Hamilton/ Penguin and at Quick Reads.

Thanks to Victoria Evaristo, Roger Robinson, Shavon Johnson, Jan Sharkey-Dodds, Dominy Roe – and to the youngsters I interviewed through them.

Thanks to the teenage readers who trawled through the text for authenticity: my god-daughter, Portia St Hilaire-Daley who told me, while rolling her eyes in exasperation, that the word 'minger is so, like, 1990s. *No one* uses it any more. Doh!', and to Akilah Cohen who corrected my street fashion *faux pas*.

Thanks to my husband David for all his support, as always.

# Quick Reads

## Short, sharp shots of entertainment

As fast and furious as an action film. As thrilling as a theme park ride. Quick Reads are short sharp shots of entertainment – brilliantly written books by bestselling authors and celebrities. Whether you're an avid reader who wants a quick fix or haven't picked up a book since school, sit back, relax and let Quick Reads inspire you.

We would like to thank all our partners in the Quick Reads project for their help and support:

Arts Council England
The Department for Business, Innovation and Skills
NIACE
unionlearn
National Book Tokens
The Reading Agency
National Literacy Trust
Welsh Books Council
Basic Skills Cymru, Welsh Assembly Government
The Big Plus Scotland
DELNI
NALA

Quick Reads would also like to thank the Department for Business, Innovation and Skills; Arts Council England and World Book Day for their sponsorship and NIACE for their outreach work.

Quick Reads is a World Book Day initiative.
www.quickreads.org.uk                www.worldbookday.com

# Quick Reads

## Books in the Quick Reads series

# Other resources

Free courses are available for anyone who wants to develop their skills. You can attend the courses in your local area. If you'd like to find out more, phone 0800 66 0800.

 Don't get by get on 0800 66 0800

A list of books for new readers can be found on www.firstchoicebooks.org.uk or at your local library.

**read**
readingagency.org.uk

Publishers Barrington Stoke (www.barringtonstoke.co.uk) and New Island (www.newisland.ie) also provide books for new readers.

Barrington Stoke

OPEN DOOR

The BBC runs an adult basic skills campaign. See www.bbc.co.uk/raw.

BBC
**raw**
skills for everyday life

www.quickreads.org.uk          www.worldbookday.com